A HOPPER CAR can carry enough grain to feed a horse for eight months.

BOXCARS often carry cows, horses, or pigs.

*To Shari, who loves trains as much as
I do, and to her new child, who will
soon be reading about them*
—P.S.

For Jane
—S.H.

I LOVE TRAINS!
Text copyright © 2001 by Philemon Sturges   Illustrations copyright © 2001 by Shari Halpern
Printed in Mexico All rights reserved.   www.harperchildrens.com   Library of Congress
Cataloging-in-Publication Data   Sturges, Philemon. I love trains! / by Philemon Sturges ;
illustrated by Shari Halpern. p.   cm. Summary: A boy expresses his love of trains,
describing many kinds of train cars and their special jobs.   ISBN 0-06-028900-7 —
ISBN 0-06-028901-5 (lib. bdg.)   [1.Railroads—Trains—Fiction.   2. Stories in rhyme.]
I. Halpern, Shari, ill.   II. Title. PZ8.3.S9227 Iae   2001   [E]—dc21   99-86367
1 2 3 4 5 6 7 8 9 10
❖
First Edition

I Love Trains!

BY **Philemon Sturges**

ILLUSTRATED BY **Shari Halpern**

HarperCollinsPublishers

Trains, trains, trains! I like trains.

I like trains that hoot and roar
as they rumble by my door.

First come engines, big and strong,

pulling lots of cars along.

Some cars keep things from the rain.

Some cars carry trucks or grain,

or cows

or hogs

or gas

or logs.

Some carry steel; some carry scrap,

or secret stuff that's under wrap.

But the best car's at the end,
and as the train goes round the bend,

I wave.

I'm glad

to see the car that carries Dad.

Trains, trains, trains!

I LOVE trains!

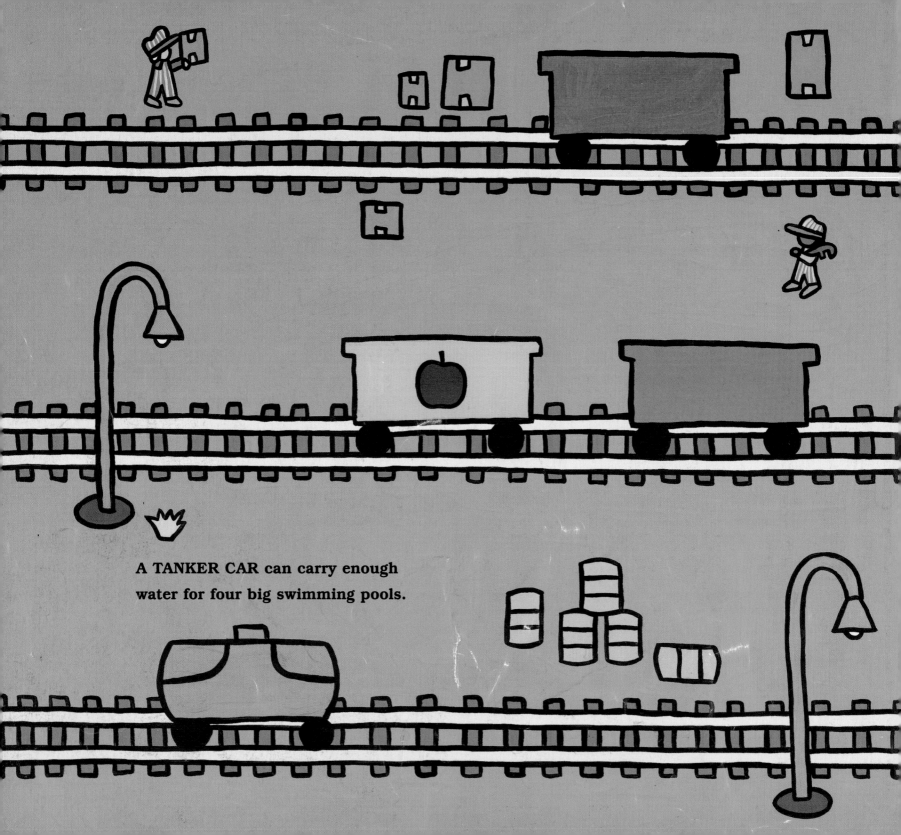

A TANKER CAR can carry enough water for four big swimming pools.